I0822834

"But certainly God has heard me;
He has attended to the voice of my prayer"
Psalm 66:19

www.ingramcontent.com/pod-product-compliance
Lightning Source LLC
Chambersburg PA
CBHW060624310726
48982CB00003B/665
* 9 7 9 8 9 8 6 8 3 5 4 0 2 *